To Lee and Diane

This book is set in Century 725/Monotype; Grilled Cheese BTN/Fontbros

Printed in China
Reinforced binding

This special edition was printed for Kohl's, Inc. (Distribution on behalf of Kohl's
Cares, LLC, its wholly owned subsidiary) by Hyperion Books for Children, an
imprint of Buena Vista Books, Inc., New York.

Kohl's
Style Number 9781368084079
Factory Number 131076
Production Date 01/2022

First Edition, September 2007
10 9 8 7 6 5 4 3 2 1
FAC-025393-22014
Library of Congress Cataloging-in-Publication Data on file.

ISBN: 978-1-368-08407-9

This title won the 2008 Theodor Seuss Geisel Award for the English U.S. Edition
published by Hyperion Books for Children, an imprint of Buena Vista Books, Inc.,
in the previous year in 2007.

Visit www.hyperionbooksforchildren.com and www.pigeonpresents.com

There Is a Bird on Your Head!

An **ELEPHANT & PIGGIE** Book
By **Mo Willems**
Hyperion Books for Children / *New York*

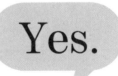

There is a bird
on my head?

aggghhh!!!

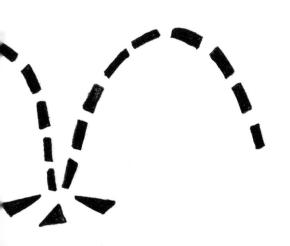

Is there a bird on my head now?

Now there are two birds on your head.

The birds on my head are in love?

19

How do you know they are love birds?

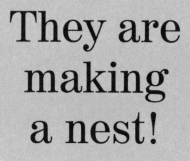

They are
making
a nest!

22

24

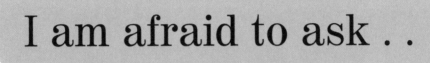

You have three eggs
on your head.

The eggs are hatching!

They have hatched.

Now, I have three baby chicks on my head!

43

I do not want three baby chicks, two birds, and a nest on my head!

Where do you want them?

49

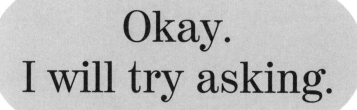

Okay.
I will try asking.

Have you read all of Elephant and Piggie's funny adventures?

Today I Will Fly!

My Friend Is Sad

I Am Invited to a Party!

There Is a Bird on Your Head!
(Theodor Seuss Geisel Medal)

I Love My New Toy!

I Will Surprise My Friend!

Are You Ready to Play Outside?
(Theodor Seuss Geisel Medal)

Watch Me Throw the Ball!

Elephants Cannot Dance!

Pigs Make Me Sneeze!

I Am Going!

Can I Play Too?

We Are in a Book!
(Theodor Seuss Geisel Honor)

I Broke My Trunk!
(Theodor Seuss Geisel Honor)

Should I Share My Ice Cream?

Happy Pig Day!

Listen to My Trumpet!

Let's Go for a Drive!
(Theodor Seuss Geisel Honor)

A Big Guy Took My Ball!
(Theodor Seuss Geisel Honor)

I'm a Frog!

My New Friend Is So Fun!

Waiting Is Not Easy!
(Theodor Seuss Geisel Honor)

I Will Take a Nap!

I *Really* Like Slop!

The Thank You Book